"HELLO READING books are a perfect introduction to reading. Brief sentences full of word repetition and full-color pictures stress visual clues to help a child take the first important steps toward reading. Mastering these storybooks will build children's reading confidence and give them the enthusiasm to stand on their own in the world of words."

—Bee Cullinan
Past President of the International Reading
Association, Professor in New York University's
Early Childhood and Elementary Education Program

"Readers aren't born, they're made. Desire is planted—planted by parents who work at it."

—Jim Trelease
author of *The Read-Aloud Handbook*

"When I was a classroom reading teacher, I recognized the importance of good stories in making children understand that reading is more than just recognizing words. I saw that children who have ready access to storybooks get excited about reading. They also make noticeably greater gains in reading comprehension. The development of the HELLO READING stories grows out of this experience."

—Harriet Ziefert
M.A.T., New York University School of Education
Author, Language Arts Module,
Scholastic Early Childhood Program

For Jon and Jamie

PUFFIN BOOKS
Published by the Penguin Group
Viking Penguin, a division of Penguin Books USA Inc.,
40 West 23rd Street, New York, New York 10010, U.S.A.
Penguin Books Ltd, 27 Wrights Lane, London W8 5TZ, England
Penguin Books Australia Ltd, Ringwood, Victoria, Australia
Penguin Books Canada Ltd, 2801 John Street, Markham, Ontario, Canada L3R 1B4
Penguin Books (N.Z.) Ltd, 182–190 Wairau Road, Auckland 10, New Zealand

Penguin Books Ltd, Registered Offices: Harmondsworth, Middlesex, England

Published in Puffin Books, 1990

1 3 5 7 9 10 8 6 4 2
Text copyright © Harriet Ziefert, 1990
Illustrations copyright © Laura Rader, 1990
All rights reserved

Library of Congress Catalog Card Number: 89-62907
ISBN: 0-14-054220-5

Printed in Singapore for Harriet Ziefert, Inc.

Follow Me!

Harriet Ziefert
Pictures by Laura Rader

PUFFIN BOOKS

"I'm going shopping,"
said Lee's mother.
"Do you want to come?"

"Okay!" said Lee.
"I'll come."

"Where are we going?"
Lee asked.

"To a big store,"
said his mother.
"I need a baby gift."

"Here we are,"
said Lee's mother.
"Follow me!"

She pushed on the door.
Then Lee pushed
and pushed until . . .

he was inside.

"Follow me!"
said Lee's mother.
"Let's ride the escalator!"

"I like the escalators,"
said Lee.
"Moving stairs are neat!"

"Be careful getting off,"
said Lee's mother.
"And follow me!"

Lee followed his mother.
She walked to the elevators.
"It will be quicker!" she said.

An elevator came.
The doors opened.
Lee's mother got on.
And then the doors closed.

Lee's mother was
on the elevator.

Lee was alone
on the 2nd floor.

"I'll follow my mother,"
said Lee to himself.
He took the next elevator.

Lee rode to the 3rd floor.
The doors opened.
And Lee got off.

Chairs

Lee did not see his mother.
He read a sign.

"My mother is not buying chairs," said Lee.

"I must follow my mother!"

So he took the
next elevator.

Lee rode to the 4th floor.

The doors opened.
And Lee got off.

Towels

Lee did not see his mother.
He read a sign.

"My mother is not buying
towels," said Lee.

"And I must follow
my mother!"

So he took the
next elevator.

Lee rode to the 5th floor.
The door opened.
And Lee got off.

Lee did not see his mother.

Babies

He read a sign.

Lee smiled and said,
"My mother needs
a gift for a new baby."

Babies →

Lee followed the sign.

And he found his mother!

"Where were you?"
she cried.

"What have you been doing?"

"I've been following you!"
said Lee with a big smile.